Milo's Big Mistake

And if you've enjoyed reading about
Little Dolphin and his adventures,
why not try reading the Little Animal Ark
books, also by Lucy Daniels?

Milo's Big Mistake

Illustrated by DAVID MELLING

LUCY DANIELS

Hodder
Children's
Books

A division of Hodder Headline Limited

To a very special boy called Jamie Morgan who likes all kinds of things but especially stones, stars, and dolphins. With much love x

Special thanks to Jan Burchett and Sara Vogler

Text copyright © 2004 Working Partners Limited
Created by Working Partners Limited, London, W6 0QT
Illustrations copyright © 2004 David Melling

First published in Great Britain in 2004
by Hodder Children's Books

The rights of Lucy Daniels and David Melling to be identified as the Author
and Illustrator of the Work respectively have been asserted by them in
accordance with the Copyright, Designs and Patents Act 1988.

10 9 8 7 6 5 4 3 2

All rights reserved. No part of this publication may be reproduced, stored in a retrieval
system, or transmitted, in any form or by any means without the prior written permission
of the publisher, nor be otherwise circulated in any form of binding or cover other than
that in which it is published and without a similar condition being imposed on the subse-
quent purchaser.

All characters in this publication are fictitious and any resemblance to real
persons, living or dead, is purely coincidental.

A Catalogue record for this book is available from the
British Library

ISBN 0 340 87348 5

Printed and bound in Great Britain by
Clays Ltd, St Ives plc

The paper and board used in this paperback by Hodder Children's
Books are natural recyclable products made from wood grown in
sustainable forests. The manufacturing processes conform to the
environmental regulations of the country of origin.

Hodder Children's Books
A division of Hodder Headline Limited
338 Euston Road, London NW1 3BH

CHAPTER ONE

"Look at me, Milo!" Little Dolphin
called to his best friend. He
flicked his tail and leaped out
of the sea. "Bet you can't jump
higher than that!" he whistled,
as he plunged down below the
surface again.

Little Dolphin and Milo were
having a jumping competition
in the middle of Urchin Bay.

They were leaping above the waves that rolled in from the ocean. Little Dolphin had only just learned how to jump, and now he wanted to do it all the time.

"Bet I *can* jump higher!" chirped Milo. "*And* I'll do a twist!"

He flipped his flippers and launched himself into the air. But suddenly, a big wave came from nowhere and knocked him into a spin!

He sank down through a shoal of mackerel, who scattered and darted away.

"What happened?" he spluttered.

"A really big wave knocked you over," Little Dolphin told him.

The two friends poked their heads above the foamy waves.

"The sky's going dark," clicked Milo. "Is it night time already?"

"Of course not!" Little Dolphin grinned. "We haven't had afternoon yet. It's just clouds blocking out the sun."

They looked up at the dark clouds as they billowed across the sky.

"And the currents are really strong too," Little Dolphin noticed. "I can feel them pulling me about."

"Fantastic!" squeaked Milo.

"We've got all afternoon to play in them! Let's get started!"

"You're right," Little Dolphin agreed. "But there's one thing you've forgotten."

Milo looked puzzled. "Let me think," he said. "I'm here. You're here. The waves are here. So what is it?"

"You're such a scatterbrain, Milo!" Little Dolphin exclaimed. "You're coming to my cave for lunch!"

"So I am!" chirped Milo. "I wondered why my tummy was making such funny noises!"

"Race you back home,"

Little Dolphin whistled. "And after lunch we'll call for Poppy. She'll love these waves!"

They sped along the reef that grew in the middle of Urchin Bay, dived under a clump of pink coral and darted inside Little Dolphin's cave.

"Slow down, you two!" clicked Little Dolphin's mum,

as she arranged lunch on the rock table. "You're making me dizzy!"

"Sorry, Mum," Little Dolphin chirped. "The waves are really high today!"

"And we want to play in them!" added Milo, gobbling down a big bite of food.

"Michael the weather fish has said there's a big storm coming," warned Little Dolphin's mum. "I'm going to store everything safely until it's gone."

"I've never seen a big storm before," Little Dolphin whistled. "What will happen?"

"There'll be heavy rain and strong winds," his mum told him as she put away her rare shell collection. "There might even be thunder and lightning," she warned. And of course, the waves will be huge."

"Wow, I can't wait!" Little Dolphin squeaked.

The two friends were so excited they swooshed around the cave sending swirls of bubbles everywhere.

"Goodness," clicked Little Dolphin's mum. "It's like having a storm right here in the cave! Go and play. But don't go too far. You could get swept away – the currents are very strong. And don't go near the old wreck. It might not be safe in this weather."

"We won't, Mum," Little Dolphin grinned. "Let's go, Milo!"

Little Dolphin and Milo dashed through the choppy water towards Poppy's house. The storm was getting nearer. Out to sea, the sky was lit with bright jagged forks of light and they could hear distant rumbles out in the bay.

Poppy the spinner dolphin was spinning madly in circles in the white-flecked waves. "Hello, you two," she clicked. "Isn't this great?"

"Do you want to come and play with us?" Little Dolphin asked.

"Yes please!" chirped Poppy, spinning even faster. "Let's play shipwrecks. I'll be a whirlpool."

"I'm the ship, then!" exclaimed

Milo. He flapped his flippers and made loud creaking noises. "I'm sinking!"

"Here comes a tidal wave!" Little Dolphin whistled. He reared up on his tail, blew a huge whoosh through his blowhole and flopped on top of his friend. He and Milo sank down through the churning water on to the sea-bed. Poppy whizzed round them, whistling with delight.

"We've sunk him!" Little Dolphin squeaked as they collapsed in the sand.

There was a strange rustling. The three friends looked to see

what it was. Then, all of a
sudden, a grumpy face poked
out from a dark cave beside
them.

It was the old conger eel,
Cornelius – and he looked
furious!

CHAPTER TWO

"How dare you make all that noise!" Cornelius growled. "It's hard enough trying to have a nap in this storm, without silly little whippersnappers like you fooling around!"

"We ... we ... we're very sorry, Mr Cornelius, sir," Little Dolphin apologised. They were outside Cornelius's cave, but nobody played near there on purpose. The stormy water must have swept them along the reef.

"Little Dolphin was pretending to be a tidal wave," explained Milo. "And I was a ship – so I had to sink."

"We were only playing," clicked Poppy nervously.

"Playing!" grunted the old eel. "You'd be better off shrimp-watching or cockle-collecting – or something else quiet. Now go away and stop disturbing me."

The three friends didn't need telling twice. They sped off as fast as they could.

"Cornelius is always so grumpy!" Little Dolphin declared, as they came to a stop on the other side of the reef. "We'd better do as he says, and keep away."

"Well I'm not going cockle-collecting," Poppy said firmly.

"Or shrimp-watching," squeaked Milo. "Let's play hide-and-seek instead!"

"Good idea," Little Dolphin chirped. "I'll count first." He closed his eyes and started to

count while Milo and Poppy
swooshed away to hide.

"... Ninety-eight, ninety-nine, one
hundred ... coming, ready or
not!" Little Dolphin called at last.
He opened his eyes and had a
quick look around. The sea was
getting rougher, and the sand
was being churned up in the
strong currents. Not a dolphin in
sight.

He knew where Poppy would
be hiding; she had a favourite
place – in the thick weed, by the
starfish caves. He made straight
for the two waving clumps of

rubbery seaweed, and poked his nose into the first one he came to.

There was Poppy among the leaves.

"How did you find me so quickly?" she squeaked in amazement.

"You always hide here!" Little Dolphin grinned.

"No, I don't!" clicked Poppy indignantly. "Sometimes I hide in the other bush."

"Well, I'm glad I've found you," Little Dolphin said. "You can help me look for Milo now."

Little Dolphin and Poppy peered into the starfish caves. There was no one there.

"Let's try the other side of the reef," Little Dolphin suggested.

They set off, swimming over a bed of sleeping oysters, then under an arch of barnacle-covered rock. Eventually, they

came to the old wrecked ship
that lay on the sea-bed.

Poppy started to swim past,
but Little Dolphin stopped. The
wreck was a very good place to
hide and he knew Milo loved
playing in it.

The old ship looked very
different in the storm. It was dark,
down amongst the rotten wood.

Little Dolphin could see seaweed on its deck, waving in the stormy currents, like the tentacles of a giant octopus. He didn't like the idea of searching in there. It was much too scary. And anyway, his mum had told him and Milo it would be dangerous to play there during the storm.

Little Dolphin turned to swim on. But all of a sudden he heard a faint squeak from the wreck.

"Help!"

It was Milo!

Little Dolphin called Poppy back. "Milo's in the wreck!" he clicked anxiously. "And my mum said we mustn't play in there today. He's so forgetful! We'd better get him out – and quickly!"

Little Dolphin and Poppy dived down through the broken wooden deck and peered into the dark, murky water. They couldn't see their friend anywhere.

"Where are you, Milo?" Little Dolphin called.

"Behind the treasure chest!" came Milo's voice. "Hurry! I'm stuck."

Little Dolphin swam towards

the big wooden chest with rusty metal hinges. Lying across the chest was a huge piece of timber. Suddenly Little Dolphin saw Milo's nose poke out from behind it. It looked very funny.

"You fooled me, Milo," Little Dolphin grinned. "For a moment, I thought you really were stuck!"

But Milo's eyes were round and wide with fear. "This isn't a joke," he squeaked. "I *am* stuck!"

CHAPTER THREE

Poor Milo! Little Dolphin was very worried!

"Behind the treasure chest seemed like such a great hiding place," clicked Milo. "I was just squeezing in when suddenly this huge plank of wood fell down in front of me."

Little Dolphin felt the currents of water racing though the holes in the wreck and making the sand swirl. His mum was right. The old ship would be dangerous in a storm. The timbers were shifting and creaking all around them.

"What's going to happen when the storm gets here?" squealed Milo in alarm. "It'll all fall down on me!"

"Don't worry, Milo," Little Dolphin said, trying to sound brave. "We'll get you out of there before you can say slithering sea snakes! Let's move this plank, Poppy."

Little Dolphin put his flipper

over one end of the plank and
Poppy swam to the other. They
tried to heave it away from the
chest, but it just wouldn't budge.
They hooked their tails round the
wood and pulled with all their
might.

Still nothing happened. The
timber was too heavy for them.

"It didn't move as much as a shrimp's whisker!" groaned Poppy. "What are we going to do?"

Little Dolphin could see Milo's frightened eyes peering out from behind the chest. He had to find a way to free his friend. "We must get help!" he whistled. "Come on, Poppy."

"Don't leave me on my own!" squeaked Milo.

"I'll stay with here with Milo," said Poppy bravely. She nuzzled Milo with her nose. "I'll keep you cheerful till Little Dolphin comes back."

"But how?" asked Milo miserably.

"Well, I know a new dance!" Poppy chirped brightly. "It's called the flip and spin. I'll show you."

"Better not!" clicked Little Dolphin hastily. "That might bring the wreck down on all of us!" He thought quickly.

"Do you remember the song we sang every day in Mrs Haddock's playgroup?" he asked.

"You mean, 'What Shall We Do With the Shrunken Pilchard'?"

asked Milo, forgetting to be scared for the moment. "That was my favourite!"

"Great!" grinned Poppy. "We'll sing it while Little Dolphin goes for help."

"OK," agreed Milo. "Don't forget the verse about the dizzy old dogfish."

"We'll sing all twenty-three verses," Poppy promised him.

"And I'll be back before you've finished!" Little Dolphin chirped. Then he shot out of the wreck.

CHAPTER FOUR

The stormy water was even
rougher now, and the old ship
was groaning and swaying.
There was no time to lose! But
where could Little Dolphin turn for
help? He swam off fast across
the bay, but no one was in sight.
Then he realised that he was
passing a cave where he knew
someone was at home.

Cornelius! He felt a sudden shiver run from his nose to his tail. Oh dear, he didn't want to disturb the grumpy conger eel again. But he had no choice! He stopped at the entrance. He didn't dare go any further. It was dark and gloomy, and he could hear a terrible rumbling noise coming from inside.

Cornelius must be waiting to pounce on anyone who came near!

Then Little Dolphin thought of poor Milo trapped in the creaking wreck, and he knew he had to be brave. He edged slowly in.

The rumbling noise echoed all around. Little Dolphin looked anxiously up and down. The sound was coming from the deepest, darkest corner. Little Dolphin swam closer, feeling very scared.

Now, at last, he could see Cornelius. The old conger eel wasn't lying in wait after all.

He was snoring!

Little Dolphin could feel his heart pounding. He would have to wake Cornelius up. He gave the old eel a gentle nudge. But Cornelius just rolled over in his sleep. Little Dolphin tapped him with his flipper. Cornelius gave a snort but he still didn't wake. "Mr Cornelius!" Little Dolphin whistled loudly. "Please wake up!"

Cornelius's beady eyes popped open and he sprang up. "What's going on?" he growled. "Who's there?"

Little Dolphin froze with fright as the conger eel stared at him.

"I'm sorry, Mr Cornelius, but—"

Cornelius whipped his tail angrily. "Sorry?" he bellowed. "Waking me up twice in one day! *You'll* be sorry, when I tell your mother!"

"But I need your help," Little Dolphin insisted.

"Help?" frowned Cornelius, swishing his tail angrily. "Is this a joke? I've told you to leave me alone. I don't want to see you anywhere near this cave again! Be off with you!"

Little Dolphin was trembling all over, but he had to make Cornelius understand. This was an emergency. "Milo's in trouble!" he squeaked. "He's stuck in the wreck! And Poppy's there with him! And they're singing songs to stay cheerful! And the storm's getting closer! And the wreck's going to squash him – and we're all so scared! Please help!"

Cornelius looked hard at him.

Oh dear, thought Little Dolphin, he thinks I've made it all up!

And then, slowly, the expression on Cornelius's face changed.

"Why didn't you say so straight away?" he said, looking worried too. "Of course I'll come with you."

"Do you know where the old wreck is, Mr Cornelius?" Little Dolphin asked timidly as they swam along though the stormy waters.

"Of course," said Cornelius. "Used to play there all the time when I was a young eel! Things were different then, you know. Us young elvers never went around waking up our elders."

"We really didn't mean any harm," Little Dolphin said.

Cornelius grunted. "Maybe not," he said gruffly.

They swam up to the old wreck. Little Dolphin could see bits of wood breaking off its sides and swirling away in the rough seas. He could hear his friends still singing. *"Put him in a barrel and roll him over ..."*

As soon as Poppy and Milo saw the old conger eel, they gulped and stopped.

"It's all right," Little Dolphin said quickly. "Mr Cornelius has come to help."

"Now then, young Milo," said Cornelius kindly. "You've got yourself into a bit of a mess, haven't you?"

Milo nodded glumly.

"We tried to move the wood," said Poppy, "but it was too heavy."

Cornelius swam up and down the length of the plank, prodding it with his nose. "It's a very solid piece of timber," he agreed. Then he turned and began to swim away.

Little Dolphin had thought Cornelius was going to help get Milo out. But instead he was leaving them! "Where are you going?" he clicked anxiously.

Cornelius stopped at the gap in the deck. "We can't shift that wood on our own," he said solemnly. "I'm going to fetch the Lobster Brigade!"

CHAPTER FIVE

"When's Cornelius coming back?" squeaked Milo, as the three friends waited for help to arrive. "He's been gone ages!"

The wreck swayed dangerously in the churning water. The storm was almost overhead now and nobody felt like singing any more.

"The Lobster Brigade station's not far away," Little Dolphin said. "He'll be back with Captain Capes and his crew as soon as he can."

All of a sudden they heard a loud blaring from a conch shell.

"It's their siren!" Poppy whistled with relief.

Cornelius appeared through the gap in the deck above. "The brigade's right behind me," he announced as he swam down to join them.

"At last!" exclaimed Milo. "I can feel the roof pressing down on me!"

A large, important-looking lobster climbed down through the hole and strutted towards them. He was wearing a yellow hat with a badge showing the words LOBSTER BRIGADE and a pair of crossed pincers on the back.

Two smiling lantern fish darted alongside him, lighting up the gloomy space under the deck with their glow. "At the double, men!" he shouted over his shoulder. "Hup, two, three, four! Hup, two, three, four!"

One by one, the Lobster Brigade appeared through the hole and dropped to the sand. Quickly they formed two straight lines and marched smartly along, shells gleaming. They each wore the Lobster Brigade hat, and the last two pulled a clamshell cart.

"HALT!" bellowed their leader.

The brigade stopped in front of Little Dolphin and Poppy, and clicked their pincers in salute.

Little Dolphin slumped to the sand with relief. If anyone could rescue Milo, it was the Lobster Brigade. Their leader stepped forward and removed his helmet.

"Captain Capes at your service!" he announced. "Now then, what have we got here?" He inspected Milo's prison and scratched his head. "Sergeant Gripper," he ordered, slapping his helmet back on, "prepare the brigade for a spot of dolphin removal!"

A crusty old lobster shuffled over to the cart. He handed ropes and hooks to the smallest

member of the brigade, who
disappeared under the huge pile.

"What are they going to do?"
squeaked Milo anxiously. "Will it
hurt?"

"Certainly not," exclaimed
Captain Capes. "Private Pinch.
Tell the young dolphin our motto."

"Sorry, sir," came a voice
from under the pile of equipment.
"Don't know, sir!"

"It's his first day, Captain," explained Sergeant Gripper. "I haven't taught him the motto yet."

"Let's hear our motto, brigade!" ordered Captain Capes.

The Lobster Brigade stood to attention. "You're safe in our claws!" they chanted.

At that moment, there was a loud rumble overhead.

Poppy shrieked and began to spin wildly round.

"Stop that at once, Miss," ordered the captain. "Get to work, everyone! There's no time to lose!"

Poppy spun to a halt. "Sorry," she clicked.

"Lights over here!" called Sergeant Gripper, clicking his pincers.

The lantern fish darted over and shone their lights at the timber that was blocking Milo's way out.

Every lobster took a hook and a rope. They screwed the hooks into the timber and knotted the ropes to them.

"Brigade, take up your positions!" ordered Captain Capes.

"Sergeant Gripper, untangle Private Pinch!"

The new recruit was hopping around, trying to untie himself from his rope. As soon as Sergeant Gripper had got him free, the lobsters took their ropes firmly in their claws. The storm currents were racing round now, and they could hear thunder crashing overhead. It didn't look as if the wreck would hold out for much longer.

"Take the strain," ordered the captain, "and HEAVE!"

The ropes tightened as the Lobster Brigade pulled as hard as they could.

Nothing happened.

They dug their claws into the sand and pulled again. The heavy timber gave a small shudder and, at last, began to move away from the chest.

Milo poked his nose through the gap. He got one flipper free, then the other. But suddenly he stopped. "My fin's stuck!" he squeaked as he struggled.

"Brigade, heave again!"

shouted Captain Capes urgently.

The lobsters gave one last heave. Milo wriggled and twisted – and burst out of his prison! Behind him the roof gave way and collapsed in a pile of broken wood.

Little Dolphin and the Lobster Brigade gave a huge gasp – and then a cheer! And Poppy,

remembering not to spin this
time, whistled loudly.

"Are you all right, Milo?"
asked Cornelius. "No cuts and
bruises?"

"I'm fine!" chirped Milo.
"Thank you, everybody. I'd never
have got out without your help!"

"All in a day's work!" said
Captain Capes, with a smart salute.

"And now my team must make the wreck safe. Lobsters at the ready! Private Pinch, where are you?"

There was an odd grunting noise behind them. They turned to see the newest member of the Lobster Brigade, bright pink in the face and still tugging on his rope. "You're safe in our claws. You're safe in our claws!" he was muttering.

The three friends swam away from the wreck with Cornelius following.

"Thank you for fetching the Lobster Brigade, Mr Cornelius," said Milo, as they stopped at Cornelius's cave.

"Little Dolphin's mum said we shouldn't go near the wreck, but I forgot! I'm such a scatterbrain! I don't know what I'd have done without you."

"Don't mention it," Cornelius grunted, looking embarrassed.

The storm was raging right overhead now and the strong underwater currents were swirling around.

"The waves will be great!" squealed Poppy. "Last one to the surface is a silly sardine!"

Milo and Poppy raced away. Little Dolphin grinned. Milo had already forgotten his ordeal. He started to follow them, but then stopped. He couldn't leave Cornelius on his own, when they were going to have such fun.

"Would you like to come and play with us, Mr Cornelius?" he asked shyly.

The old eel looked at him for a moment. Then something very strange happened. Cornelius smiled!

"I do believe I would enjoy that," he exclaimed. "Now don't forget what Poppy said – last one to the surface is a silly sardine!"

And Little Dolphin and
Cornelius raced up to join the
others and bounce around in the
waves.